THE CLUE AT
COPPER HARBOR

A Michigan Lighthouse Adventure

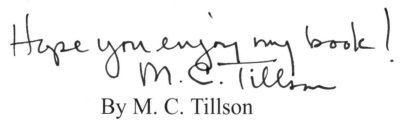

Hope you enjoy my book!
M. C. Tillson

By M. C. Tillson

Illustrated by Lisa T. Bailey

For Micah,
my best fan

to Lisa as always,
to Lloyd and Fran who were there from the start,
and to all my friends and encouragers
at Eisenhower.

THE CLUE AT COPPER HARBOR

Copyright © 2005 by M. C. Tillson

ISBN 978-0-9764824-0-6

A LIGHTHOUSE ADVENTURE BOOK
Published by A&M Writing and Publishing
Santa Clara, California
www.amwriting.com

Printed in the U.S.A
First printing, April 2005
Fourth printing, December 2016

Contents

Psst...Over Here!

As you might know, in a fictional story, the characters are made up, and that is certainly the case with Sam and Becky and their friends and family, the characters in this book. (I must add that Ranger Leslie, especially, is not at all like the real folks who take care of the Copper Harbor Lighthouse!)

Even though Becky, Sam, and the others are made up, the lighthouse, the town of Copper Harbor, Michigan, and (unfortunately) the shipwrecks are all very real. When I describe these things in my story, I use the most accurate information I know. I hope you enjoy this blend of fiction and facts (also called realistic fiction).

Copper Harbor, Michigan, 1999

I first saw the Copper Harbor Lighthouse with my friend Fran and my son Micah in 1999. We were visiting our friends, Lloyd, Clyde, Isabel, and Jim Wescoat who live in Copper Harbor, a small town on the tip of Michigan's Upper Peninsula. It was during that visit that Fran and I saw our first Northern Lights. It was pure magic—something I'll always remember!

I fell in love with Copper Harbor and the whole area during that short visit. A few years later, I was lucky enough to visit again. (It was the summer of 2002, and this time I got to share the magic with the rest of my family. They were *not* disappointed.)

After my second visit to Copper Harbor, I knew that I needed to write a book about it. It had quickly become an important place in my heart and

I wanted to share it with others. So, enjoy this book, learn a little about a special place called Copper Harbor, and see if you can find some of the magic I experienced there.

Do You Know These Words?

I love words—which is a good thing since I'm a writer. (That would be a little weird if I didn't like words, wouldn't it?)

Sometimes I use words that not all of my readers know. Most of the time you can figure out what the word means because of how and where it's used in a sentence or paragraph (that's called *context*). However, sometimes the word is used by itself or without much context, and it's difficult to figure it out.

To help you out, I thought I'd give you a **definition** or two along the way. (I've also included how to pronounce the word in parenthesis.) So,

DEFINITION
(def-i-NI-shun)
What a word means. You can find definitions for a word in a dictionary.

whenever you see a word printed in bold type (like the word definition above), look around on the same page for an explanation of what that word means.

Check It Out

There are many wonderful books and websites about lighthouses in general and about the lighthouses of the Great Lakes in particular. I've included a list of some of my favorites for you at the end of this book.

Chapter 1
MOOSE TRACKS IN
COPPER HARBOR

Sam couldn't believe his ears. His dad must be imagining things. "You're looking for what?"

"Moose tracks," said Dad. "Slow down, Alice. I know I saw some along here somewhere."

Sam and his older sister Becky looked at each other and giggled as their mom slowed the car to a crawl. Dad was leaning out the window of the car and squinting at the little shops they passed on the main street of Copper Harbor, Michigan.

"Wait! Stop! Here it is! I knew I'd seen moose tracks! Pull over, Alice!"

"But Dad," said Becky, "I don't think a moose would be hanging around stores in the middle of town. Aunt Isabel said they were shy and mostly lived farther north—up toward Canada—so I don't think..."

"Follow me," said Dad in a whisper.

Becky and Sam shrugged and got out of the car. They followed Dad into a tiny store.

"I *knew* I was right!" said Dad as he raised his arms triumphantly. "See? Moose tracks!"

"Dad," said Sam in an embarrassed whisper, "it's an ICE CREAM store."

As it turned out, Moose Tracks® was a flavor of ice cream that combined chocolate peanut butter cups with Moose Tracks fudge in vanilla ice cream. Dad and Becky both ordered Moose Tracks in waffle cones, Mom went for the Cowpacinno in a cup, and Sam decided to try the chocolate **Yooper** Mudslide in a chocolate-dipped sugar cone.

So now, Sam and Becky were sitting on a bench, on a dock, at the west end of Copper Harbor, eating their ice cream and waiting to board the

YOOPER
(U-per)
A "U.P.-er."
Someone who lives on Michigan's Upper Peninsula.

boat that would take them across the water to the Copper Harbor Lighthouse. Their mom (Alice) and dad (Mike) were inside the office of Copper Harbor Lighthouse Tours buying tickets and (no doubt) chatting with everyone inside about the history of the tiny town and its lighthouse.

"How many lighthouses do you think we'll have to see before they can finish writing their book?" asked Sam turning his chocolate-dipped cone so his tongue could catch the drop of ice cream dribbling down the side.

Becky thought for a minute as she took a bite out of her waffle cone. "I don't know. We've only been on vacation for three days and this is our fourth lighthouse. That's a little more than one lighthouse a day. We're supposed to be on vacation for three weeks which would mean…oh no! Twenty-one lighthouses!"

"No way!" groaned Sam. "There is no way I can take visiting twenty-one lighthouses. What are we going to do?"

"What are you going to do about what?" asked Mom as she walked up behind Sam waving four tickets. "We're almost ready to get on board. Captain Pete said we were the only ones on this trip so we can spend as much time as we want at the lighthouse. Isn't that wonderful? Where did your father go? He's going to be thrilled. Oh, there he is, back at the car. Yoo hoo! Mi-ike, oh Mi-ike!"

She waved her arms at their father who had his head in the trunk of their rented car. "Wait 'til he hears! I'll be right back. Don't leave without us! Yoo hoo! Mi-ike!"

Becky watched her mother calling and yoo-hooing and waving her way across the parking area toward their father. She looked at Sam and shook her head. "It's going to be a *really* long summer," she said.

A Michigan Lighthouse Adventure

Chapter 2
ON COPPER HARBOR

"Where are you folks from?" asked Captain Pete as he carefully slipped his boat, the *Virginia Gray*, away from the dock and out into the harbor.

Dad turned to talk to the captain. "We're from California. Near San Francisco. Have you ever been out that way?"

"Nope, I never made it that far. Actually I was on my way to visit a friend in California when I stopped up here to see my cousin. I fell in love with the place and never wanted to go anywhere else."

"Better be careful up there, son." the captain continued. "The water's a bit choppy and you never know when one of those big waves will…"

As the captain spoke, a huge wave slammed over the **bow** of the boat and drenched Sam.

"Yep, just like that. Sorry about that, young man. There's a towel under the seat there."

BOW
(rhymes with "cow")
The front, pointy part of a boat.

Becky took one look at Sam and laughed out loud. Water from the big wave dripped down his hair, his nose, and even his ears. His shirt was soaked. "Why don't you just swim all the way to the lighthouse Sam?" she laughed. "I don't think *anybody* could be any wetter than you are. You look like. . ."

But Sam never found out what he looked like because just at that moment, another wave came over the side of the boat and swamped Becky.

Sam exploded with laughter. "Actually Becky, I think you just proved that somebody *can* be wetter than me. Just look at you. Your shirt is all wet— even your eyelashes are dripping!"

Captain Pete grinned at the two of them. "Like I was saying, you never can tell when one of those big waves will come along and get you wet—especially when young Tom Adams is helping out."

Becky looked around the boat, but saw only her family and Captain Pete. "Who's Tom Adams?" she asked. "I don't see anybody else around here."

Captain Pete was quiet for a minute and then he cleared his throat. "Well, if the truth be known, you can't exactly see Tom. He's…well, to be honest…uh, Tom is a…uh…well, Tom is a ghost."

"A ghost!" echoed Sam and Becky.

"Now don't be frightened, Tom's not a bad ghost, but he *can* cause a little trouble from time to time. And he loves to get people wet when they're riding out to the lighthouse."

"But…" sputtered Sam.

"How can…" Becky started.

But Captain Pete interrupted them both. "Well here we are—right on time!" He pulled the Lighthouse Tours boat alongside the dock below the Copper Harbor Lighthouse. A young woman in a park ranger's uniform stood waiting for them.

"Be careful now, and don't slip getting out. I'll be back for you around 5:30. Leslie here will take care of you until then."

One after another, Mom, Dad, Sam, and Becky stepped out of the boat and climbed the short ladder to the dock. As Becky turned to thank the captain, he winked. "Keep your eyes open and your mouth closed," he said in a soft voice that only Becky could hear.

Before Becky could ask him what he was talking about, Captain Pete pushed away from the dock and headed the *Virginia Gray* back across the harbor towards town.

Chapter 3
LEARNING THE HARD WAY

"What did Captain Pete say to you?"

"What?"

"The captain," said Sam. "I saw him say something to you when you got off the boat just now. Was it about the ghost?"

"Yes, it was. He said…" Becky stopped and looked up as the young woman in the park ranger's uniform came over to them.

"Hi, I'm Leslie," the woman said. "I'm a park ranger here at the Copper Harbor Lighthouse and I couldn't help overhearing your conversation. Did Captain Pete tell you his old story about the ghost that's supposed to haunt the lighthouse?"

"Yes, he did!" said Sam. "The captain said the ghost's name was Tom Adams and that he sometimes caused trouble around the lighthouse and in the boats and..."

Ranger Leslie gave a polite little laugh and patted Sam on the head. "Well, I'll tell you what I tell all the folks who ride over with Captain Pete. I've worked at the Copper Harbor Lighthouse for five years now and I have never seen, heard, or felt

FIGMENT
(FIG-mint)
Something you imagined.

a ghostly presence on the grounds. I'm afraid that Captain Pete's ghost is a **figment** of his imagination— a little treat he conjures up for the visitors. Now come with me and I'll give you some real facts about the lighthouse."

Ranger Leslie walked ahead to answer a question for Mom and Dad. Sam and Becky trailed behind and said nothing, but in spite of Ranger Leslie's casual dismissal, they kept their eyes open for anything unusual.

"In 1844, the *John Jacob Astor* was shipwrecked in Copper Harbor." Ranger Leslie began her talk standing by the fireplace in the main room of what had been the first Copper Harbor Lighthouse. The building had since been turned into a museum that was home to many fascinating **exhibits**.

EXHIBITS
(egg-ZIB-itz)
The displays in a museum that give information. Exhibits might be signs and posters on the wall, special programs on a computer, or a collection of items to examine.

Out the back door of the museum and farther up the path was the lighthouse that was built after the first one was torn down. This lighthouse was also a museum and had been restored to the way it looked when the lighthouse keeper and his family lived there in 1866.

Outhouse

Lighthouse Keeper's
Restored House
(built in 1866)

Lighthouse Museum
(original lighthouse-
built in 1848)

As Sam and Becky stood at the back of the room and listened with their mom and dad, Ranger Leslie continued her talk about lighthouses and shipwrecks in a dull, plodding, monotone voice that held absolutely no hope of excitement.

"The need for a lighthouse at Copper Harbor was documented as early as 1845 by the author John R. St. John in his writings. At about the same time, copper was discovered on the Keweenaw Peninsula, bringing more ships to the area and making it even more important to improve the navigational aids that guided these ships.

"With the completion of the Soo Locks on St. Marys River in 1855, ships could travel from Lake Superior to the other Great Lakes and on to the Atlantic Ocean. Shipping became an important industry to the Keweenaw Peninsula, and lighthouses were critical to the shipping industry."

Sam and Becky tried to pay attention to what Ranger Leslie was saying, but her voice made them sleepy. "In 1847, President James Polk and the United States Congress approved $5,000 to build a lighthouse at Copper Harbor…"

Sam shifted from one foot to the other and Becky leaned against the wall. From her spot by the door, Becky could just see the

blinking lights and colorful exhibits in the next room. Was Ranger Leslie *ever* going to stop?

But Leslie plodded on. "As the copper boom continued, the number of ships on Lake Superior increased and so did the need for more lighthouses. Shipwrecks were on the rise. Just in the waters around the Keweenaw Peninsula, many ships were lost, including: the *John Jacob Astor*, the *City of Bangor*, the *Langham*— which was originally **christened** the *Tom Adams*, the *Maplehurst*…"

"Did you hear that?" whispered Becky to Sam.

"Tom Adams is the name of the ghost Captain Pete told us about!" he replied.

CHRISTENED
(KRIS-sind)
When a boat is given its name.

"Come on!" Becky grabbed Sam's hand, and without another word, they tiptoed to the door and slipped outside. Ranger Leslie continued to talk— with Mom and Dad listening intently to her every word. No one even noticed that Becky and Sam were gone.

Chapter 4
LEARNING MADE EASY

"Did you hear that? Tom Adams was the name of the ghost that Captain Pete told us about!" said Sam. He and Becky were standing just outside the back entrance of the lighthouse museum.

"I know, I know," said Becky. "But according to Ranger Leslie, *Tom Adams* is…or was the name of a ship that sank. The *Langham* used to be called the *Tom Adams*, right? I don't understand, do you? Do you think the ghost is a ship?"

"Yes. I mean, no. I mean, yes, Ranger Leslie said the *Langham* was first called the *Tom Adams* and no, I don't understand either," said Sam. "I thought Captain Pete said Tom Adams was a boy."

"Me too," agreed Becky. She thought for a minute. "Don't you think it's strange that all of a sudden we've heard the name Tom Adams from two different people in less than an hour? That's a pretty big coincidence."

"It *is* weird. I think we should find out more about Tom Adams. I heard Ranger Leslie say there was some stuff about shipwrecks in the museum. I'm going to see if I can find out more about the shipwreck of the *Tom Adams*."

"Good idea," said Becky, "and while you're doing that, I'll go over to the lighthouse keeper's house and see if I can find out anything over there. I'll meet you back here in twenty minutes."

"OK," said Sam and while Becky headed up the path to the lighthouse keeper's house, he slipped back into the museum to take a look around.

The museum building had been the original Copper Harbor Lighthouse, but when it was built in 1848, the builders used such flimsy materials that the building didn't last very long. In 1866, it was completely torn down. Some of the rocks from its **foundation** were used to build a new lighthouse nearby.

FOUNDATION
(fown-DAY-shun)
The solid structure on which a building is built.

In 1919, the U.S. Government decided to make the Copper Harbor Lighthouse into an automatic light that turned on and off by itself. There was no longer any need for a lighthouse keeper to turn the light off during the day, and on at night and during fog and storms.

In early 1957, the State of Michigan bought the lighthouse property from the U.S. Coast Guard for $5,000. The state made the property part of Fort Wilkins State Park and turned the original lighthouse keeper's house into a museum with exhibits about lighthouses, shipwrecks, copper mining, and Copper Harbor.

Sam looked around at all the maps and charts and pictures on display, and then he saw the exhibit about shipwrecks. The exhibit used a computer to tell visitors about the shipwrecks that had happened on the **Great Lakes**. He grabbed a piece of paper and a pencil from a nearby table and sat down at the computer. He used the computer mouse to select a map of Michigan's Upper Peninsula. Then he clicked another button that put markers on the map to show where ships had been lost.

GREAT LAKES
(grayt lakes)
The five fresh-water lakes in North America, connected by the St. Lawrence seaway and ending at Niagra Falls. The names of the Great Lakes are Huron, Ontario, Michigan, Erie, and Superior (just think HOMES).

Sam searched through the names of the ships—there were so many—until he spotted what he was looking for. He clicked on the name *Langham* and read the following:

"The *Langham* (originally christened the *Tom Adams*) was making a routine run up to Port Arthur, Ontario with a load of coal when it encountered a ferocious storm on Lake Superior. The ship found shelter in **Bete Grise Bay**, on the south side of the Keweenaw Peninsula, but mysteriously caught fire early the next morning. The crew abandoned ship and, from the shore, watched their ship sink below the water. There was no loss of life.*"

BETE GRISE BAY (bay-de-GREE bay) A sheltered inlet of Lake Superior on the south side of the Keweenaw Peninsula. ("Bete Grise" means "gray beast" in French.)

The asterisk (*) beside the description meant that there was something else that needed to be mentioned. Sam clicked on the asterisk to see the note: "*It is rumored that the *Langham* carried a stowaway, a boy who had sneaked onto the ship without the captain's knowledge. But no one was ever found. Some say that the boy left town after he abandoned ship with the other crew members, but some people believe he died in the fire."

Sam looked up as some other visitors entered the room. Evidently they had already heard Ranger Leslie's talk about the history of the lighthouse and were more interested in the exhibits.

One woman came over to the computer where Sam was working. She had white hair, beautiful green eyes, and she carried a walking stick that was carved to look like a cat. She watched as Sam clicked on the different shipwrecks. When he stopped to read about the wreck of the *Langham*, she stepped closer.

"Do you want to try it out?" Sam asked the woman. But when he turned in his seat to see if she wanted to take a turn at the computer, there was no one there, and the door to the outside was standing wide open.

"Guess not," Sam muttered as he turned back to the computer.

A breeze from outside blew some of Sam's papers off the table. He reached down to pick them up, and then turned back to the computer. There, on the keyboard, he saw another piece of paper—only this one wasn't his. It was a note written in all capital letters on very old-looking paper, and it contained only two words:

HELP ME

A Michigan Lighthouse Adventure

Chapter 5
THE LIGHTHOUSE KEEPER'S HOUSE

Becky watched Sam go back into the museum, and then she walked down the path to the lighthouse keeper's house and stepped through the doorway. It was as if she had gone back in time about 140 years.

The house had been completely restored to look the way it looked in 1866—the year it was built. The back door opened into a kitchen that had a woodstove for cooking and baking, a table for preparing meals, and a pantry closet with shelves for storing food.

On one side of the room was a wooden sink with a pump instead of a faucet. The lighthouse family brought water into the house by moving the pump's long handle up and down and letting the water run into the wooden sink. It was a wonderful convenience (at the time) and the closest thing they had to running water. (It certainly was better than having to bring water into the house one bucket at a time!)

There were no bathrooms in the house, but just down the path outside the kitchen, Becky could see what she thought was an outhouse.

Becky walked through the kitchen into the next room, called the sitting room. A rocking chair sat close to another woodstove, and a doll with a **porcelain** head and long skirts sat in a small chair made of sticks and woven grass.

PORCELAIN
(POR-sah-lin)
A hard, smooth, white material made from special clay. Used to make dishes and the heads, arms, and legs of dolls.

A shelf on the wall held three very old books, and a fourth book, an alphabet book showing letters and pictures, was open on the floor. Blocks on the faded rug in front of the woodstove created a small fort around six small metal soldiers.

The children who had lived here were obviously younger than she and Sam, but it was still interesting to see how they might have spent a cold winter afternoon. Becky could almost feel the warmth of the stove as she imagined how it would be to have this lighthouse as a home.

Across from the sitting room, Becky saw stairs leading up to the lighthouse tower. She started toward the steps, but stopped suddenly when she heard something crackle under her sandal. She looked down and saw a piece of very old-looking paper that someone had dropped on the floor.

"That's weird," Becky said to herself as she bent down to pick up the paper. "I didn't see anything on the floor a few minutes ago." The paper was blank on the first side, so Becky turned it over to look at the back. There, in all capital letters, someone had written two words:

HELP ME

Chapter 6
HELP ME!

With the note in her hand, Becky dashed down the steps and out of the lighthouse keeper's house to find Sam. She saw him hurrying up the path toward her.

"Very funny Sam," she called to him. "Ha, Ha, Ha. Ho, Ho, Ho. It was such a funny joke that I almost forgot to laugh! The only thing I can't figure out is how you got over to the lighthouse keeper's house and back so quickly."

"Me?" Sam said in amazement, "what about you? Did you ever actually go to the lighthouse keeper's house or did you just pretend to go and then write your little note? The only thing *I* can't figure out is how you got back to that shipwreck exhibit in the museum without my seeing you."

"What are you talking about, Sam? I didn't write a note. I *found* the note that *you* wrote. And, I have to say your handwriting could use a little work."

"*You* found a note! I'm talking about the note that I found on the computer keyboard. VERY funny. Like I was going to fall for that. By the way, where did you find that weird paper?"

"Wait a minute," said Becky. "I'm totally confused. I was getting ready to go up the steps to the lighthouse tower when I stepped on this paper." Becky pushed the note under Sam's nose. "What's the big idea? I thought you were going to find out more about the shipwrecks on Lake Superior."

"I was," sputtered Sam, "I mean, I will. I mean, I *did*. I used this great computer program and found out a lot about the *Langham*—the ship that used to be called the *Tom Adams*. I was writing some stuff down, when this lady came over and started watching me. She seemed really interested and I thought maybe she wanted to use the computer. But when I turned around to ask her, she was gone.

"The woman left the door to the outside open, and the wind blew my papers to the floor. I reached down to pick them up, and when I looked back at the computer, this note was on the keyboard." Sam held out the note he had found.

"What does your note say?" asked Becky.

"All it says is 'HELP ME'" said Sam.

Becky swallowed. "That's the same thing mine says."

Another group of lighthouse visitors was wandering up the path, reading about the points of interest and chattering about their smooth boat trip across Copper Harbor.

Becky grabbed Sam's arm and whispered. "Let's get out of here!"

The two ran down the trail away from the lighthouse. They followed it through the brush and down to the shore of Lake Superior. There they climbed on the big rocks at the edge of the lake, and then stopped to catch their breath. At their feet was a shallow pool where a **vein** of native copper

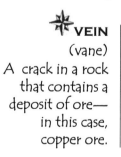
VEIN
(vane)
A crack in a rock that contains a deposit of ore—in this case, copper ore.

running through a crack in the rocks was clearly visible under the crystal clear water.

"OK," said Sam. "Let's take a look at the notes."

They put the notes side by side: the handwriting, the paper, and the words were exactly the same.

"Sam," said Becky, "if you didn't write the notes, and I didn't write the notes, then who did?"

Chapter 7
HELP WHO?

"So, Sam, who do you think wrote these strange notes?"

"And," said Sam, "where did they get this paper and why do they write so weird and…"

"And most important," interrupted Becky, "why does this person need help?"

"Maybe…" said Sam slowly, "maybe it's not a real person. At least, not anymore."

"Are you saying…"

"You have to admit that we would have noticed a real person leaving these notes. But if a ghost had left them…"

"Oh, come on, Sam," said Becky. "Do you really believe that a ghost wrote us notes?"

"Don't you?"

"I really don't know *what* to think." She paused for a minute. "Do you think we should tell Mom and Dad?"

"Well, if it *is* a ghost, it's not like he's in real danger—I mean what's the worst thing that could happen to a ghost—he's already dead, right?"

Becky giggled. "Well, that's true... So, I wonder why he needs our help."

"Why do we keep saying 'he'? How do we know the ghost is a boy? Maybe it's a girl ghost."

"I'm just assuming that it's the ghost of Tom Adams…don't you think so?"

"I don't know," said Sam slowly.

"I don't know either, " said Becky, "but I do think it's pretty interesting that Captain Pete tells us about a ghost, and then an hour later we get these very strange notes."

"So what are we going to do? Should we just ignore the notes?"

"Well, I don't know how we're going to help, do you?"

"Not really." Sam was quiet for a minute. "But I was thinking that we should try. Don't you think so?"

"I do, but I..."

"Becky, look!"

Becky turned around to see where Sam was pointing. There, floating on the pool of water at the base of the big rocks, was a piece of paper. It was the same kind of paper that the other notes were written on.

Becky scrambled down and pulled the note out of the water. Sam came over to stand beside her as she shook out the wet paper. There, written in a now-familiar handwriting, were the words:

SOLVE THE RIDDLE

Chapter 8
FIND THE RIDDLE

"Solve the riddle? What riddle? I don't get it."

Sam sat down on the big rocks and leaned back on his hands. "Who needs help, how are we supposed to help, and how can we solve a riddle we don't even have?"

"Maybe the way we're supposed to help is to solve the riddle," offered Becky.

"Terrific," said Sam. "That takes care of *that* mystery. The only question now is WHAT RIDDLE? I mean, there are millions and billions of riddles in the world. Which riddle are we supposed to solve?"

Becky and Sam were quiet for a minute—listening to the lake lapping at the rocks. Then Becky spoke.

"Since we found the notes at the lighthouses, maybe it's a riddle that has something to do with them. Maybe it's a riddle from the kids who used to live in the lighthouse. I did see some books in the sitting room exhibit. Maybe one of them was a book of riddles."

"Well what are we waiting for?" Sam jumped off the rocks and took off running down the trail toward the lighthouse. Becky was right behind him.

They were breathless by the time they arrived at the lighthouse keeper's house. Becky led the way through the kitchen to the sitting room exhibit.

"The book on the floor is an ABC book," said Becky, "but what's on the shelves?"

"It's a little hard to see the titles from here," said Sam. "There's a Bible, something called a *McGuffy's Reader*, and *A Tale of Two Cities*.

"Boy, do you think those are the only books they had?" Sam was thinking of the bookshelves full of books that had always been part of their home. He couldn't imagine having only three books to choose from. "None of those look like riddle books," he whispered to Becky.

Becky was disappointed. "You're right. There aren't any riddles here. Let's go."

She and Sam waited while a group of tourists wandered in through the kitchen door. Becky held the door open for a woman with white hair and bright green eyes who carried a beautifully carved walking stick. Sam recognized the woman as the one who had watched him gather information about the *Langham* from the computer. He smiled a greeting, but the woman quickly looked away and hurried into the house.

As they walked slowly back to the big rocks, Becky said, "This is going to be tough. It's not like riddles are scratched on the rocks or carved on all the trees. Where are we going to find the riddle he's talking about?"

"So you *do* think it's Tom Adams' ghost, don't you?"

"Honestly? I don't know what to think, but that would make the most sense...that is, if you can say that any of this makes sense."

Sam climbed the big rocks and looked out at the lake. The wind had died down and right now Lake Superior was completely flat and smooth—not even a ripple. It was very different from earlier that morning when they had crossed the harbor with Captain Pete.

"Think, think, think! If you were a riddle out here, where would you be?"

Becky sat down beside Sam and wrapped her arms around her knees. She rested her chin on her arms and sighed.

All of the sudden the wind started blowing. The lake which had been so smooth only a minute ago was now rolling and churning with white-capped waves that slapped up against the big rocks.

"Funny thing you should mention riddles," said a voice behind them.

Becky and Sam jumped and looked around to see the old woman from the lighthouse keeper's house standing right behind them on the rocks. How had she managed to climb up on the rocks without making a sound?

The woman's brilliant white hair had, at some point, been caught up in a bun, but now it was blowing wildly around her head. Her face was tan and wrinkled, and she had piercing green eyes. She wore a heavy skirt, a jacket, and sturdy walking shoes, and she carried a walking stick that was elegantly carved to look like a sleek cat.

Although her appearance was that of an older woman, her voice was young and strong. There was something a little strange about the combination— they just didn't go together.

"I did hear you talking about riddles, didn't I?" Without waiting for an answer, the old woman continued. "There is, as you said, nothing carved on the trees out here. The rangers wouldn't like it and I dare say the trees wouldn't appreciate it either. But you *did* see the riddle in the old outhouse, didn't you?"

"A riddle?" Sam jumped to his feet.

"In the outhouse?" asked Becky.

"Yes, in the outhouse. When the State of Michigan was restoring this place, they took great care to return everything to the way it was in 1866. When they got to the outhouse, they found that someone had carved a riddle into the back of the door. I guess it gave the occupants something to think about while they were…well, you know…while they were doing, er…ah…doing whatever they needed to do."

Sam and Becky looked at each other and grinned. They jumped off the rocks and raced toward the old lighthouse. "Thank you," they yelled over their shoulders at the old woman.

"You're more than welcome, my dears," the old woman said to herself. "It was my very, *very* great pleasure." And then she laughed a low laugh, tucked the walking stick up under her arm, and jumped easily from the rocks to the shore.

Chapter 9
IN THE OUTHOUSE

Sam and Becky ran as fast as they could down the trail toward the lighthouse. They were out of breath when they reached the spot where the trail crossed the path from the museum.

To the right was the restored lightkeeper's house, in front of them was the path to the museum, and to the left was the outhouse that had served as the only toilet facility available to the lighthouse keeper's family in 1866.

This particular outhouse was a favorite of tourists because (as Ranger Leslie had explained) it had not one, not two, but three seats in it—one of which was a small size made especially for children.

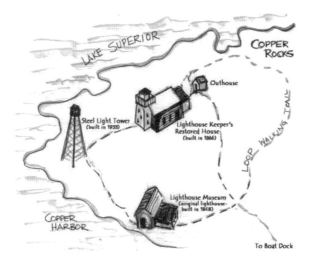

The door to the outhouse opened inward and was open to let the tourists take a peek. Sam and Becky couldn't see the back of the door, so they waited patiently while the current group of visitors went in to inspect the brightly white-washed little house.

Finally the group of tourists moved on to visit the kitchen, and Sam and Becky stepped into the outhouse and closed the door. Sure enough, on the back of the door, someone had carved these words:

If you say my name I am gone. Who am I?

* * * * *

"Sa-am...Bec-ky. The last boat will be here in just a few minutes. It's time to go." Their mother was calling from just outside the museum.

"Quick," said Sam, "write it down just the way it looks on the door. Here's some paper. Hurry!" he added as his mother called their names again. Becky quickly copied down the words as they had been carved on the back of the outhouse door so long ago.

"Samuel! Rebecca! We have to go NOW!"

Sam and Becky knew from the tone of their mom's voice that they needed to go at once—no more excuses. Becky wrote down the last word of the riddle, and then she and Sam flew down the path to the dock where the *Virginia Gray* was already loading passengers.

Becky and Sam were the last people to board the boat. It was only then that they noticed Captain Pete was nowhere to be seen. Instead, a young man in a yellow slicker was at the wheel.

"Hi," said Sam. "Are you our captain?"

"That's right, mate. I'm Captain Jack. Welcome aboard."

Where's Captain Pete?" Becky asked the young captain once the boat was underway. "We had some questions to ask him."

"Oh, you know the Captain do you? Well, I'm afraid the captain won't be answering questions for a while—he's got no voice. Must be that lar-reen-gy-tis or some such thing."

"Laryngitis? But he was talking to us just this morning." Sam was puzzled.

"Well," said Captain Jack, "it's a strange thing. One minute he's hale and hearty, swapping tales with the rest of us, and the next—well, right now he's got no voice at all. Can't even whisper his name so's anybody can hear him. If I didn't know better, I'd say somebody put a spell on old Captain Pete to keep him quiet. (He *is* a bit of a talker, you know.) It's just odd how it came on so sudden-like…just strange it is.

"Any-who, I told him I'd take over the lighthouse boat trips until he could talk again. So if you have any questions, I'll be happy to answer them for you—if I can."

"Thanks, Captain Jack," said Becky. "I think that's the only question we have for you right now. Tell Captain Pete we hope he feels better soon."

Chapter 10
FOUR FOR DINNER

That night, Sam and Becky and their parents ate at Copper Harbor's famous Harbor Haus Restaurant. The restaurant sat right on the shore of the lake and was famous for its excellent and sometimes very different food.

Sam and Becky and their mom and dad sat beside the window and watched the beginning of what would be a beautiful sunset over Lake Superior.

As they were waiting for their food, Sam glanced at Becky and then said, "Mom, Dad, I have a riddle for you." Becky gave him a sharp kick under the table, but he ignored her and continued.

"It goes like this: 'If you say my name I am gone. Who am I?' Have you ever heard that riddle? Do you know the answer?"

✳ **SAMPLER**
(SAM-plar)
A piece of embroidery (decorative sewing) showing different stitches and patterns.

"Hmmm," said his mother, "that sounds like one of those old riddles that children used to copy over and over on their slates or that young ladies cross-stitched on a **sampler**."

"I know. We think it's a really old riddle, that's why I thought you guys might know the answer— since you're so old." Sam looked at his parents with a twinkle in his eye.

"Thanks, son," said his Dad. "I'll remember that the next time we old folks go for ice cream. We'll just have to leave you young whipper-snappers at home. Hmmm. . . 'If you say my name. . . ' I don't know anything that fits that description. How about you, Alice?"

"Well, I do know that if you say Sam's name together with a chore that needs to be done, *he'll* be gone in two seconds."

"Aw, Mom, that's not the answer, " protested Sam with a smile. "C'mon now, do you know the answer to my riddle?"

"No, but I do know 'What's black and white and red all over?' Does that help?"

"Oh, I know! I know!" said Dad stabbing his arm in the air. "Pick me! Pick me! I know the

answer to that one! It's a newspaper! No, wait, it's a sunburned zebra! No, wait..."

Sam rolled his eyes at Becky and shook his head. "They're useless," he said with a grin. But before Becky could agree, the waitress arrived with their food.

Becky and Sam had both decided to experiment with a new (at least new to them) dish—fresh lake trout, grilled with a special orange sauce. According to their waitress, the trout had been caught in Copper Harbor that very morning!

"Mmmmm," said Sam as he tasted the first bite. "This is really good. You're right, Mom. This *is* better than getting chicken nuggets all the time."

Becky waited for Sam to continue probing about the riddle, but soon realized he was too distracted by the delicious dinner. It was time for *her* to take over the investigation.

"So, what are we doing tomorrow?" asked Becky. "Are we going back to the Copper Harbor Lighthouse?"

"Well, " said Mom, "I have a couple of more questions that I need answers to, but I'm pretty sure that I can find them on the Internet. So your father and I decided that we don't need to go back to the lighthouse tomorrow."

"What?!" cried Becky.

"We have to go back!" Sam sputtered at the same time. He choked on the water he was drinking and it almost came out his nose.

"I thought you kids were tired of all the lighthouses," said Mom. "We thought it would be a treat for you to skip a day before we went on to another lighthouse. We could go tour Fort Wilkins or go on a canoe ride on Lake Fanny Hooe."

"I don't want to see an old fort, " said Sam crossly.

"And I don't want to go for a dumb canoe ride, " said Becky. "We want to go back to the lighthouse and look around some more. We were just starting to have a good time."

"Yeah," said Sam. "There's still some stuff about the lighthouse that we haven't…uh…figured out and we need more time to explore."

"Well, " said Dad, "I have to admit…Ranger Leslie certainly knows her lighthouses. I could talk with her for days. She told Mom and me some of the most fascinating details about lighthouses.

"For example, did you know that in 1909 the U.S. Government gave responsibility for the nation's lighthouses to a new Lighthouse Service Bureau?

"A man named George R. Putnam was in charge of this group, and he decided it was time to automate the lighthouses so they could turn on (at sunset) and turn off (at sunrise) all by themselves. In 1919, they automated the Copper Harbor Lighthouse with a new light that flashed every 2.7 seconds and could be seen 15 miles away. So..." Dad paused for a sip of water.

"So...can we go back to the Copper Harbor Lighthouse tomorrow?" interrupted Becky gently even though she knew it wasn't polite to do so. (Sometimes when Dad got going on his stories, you simply had to interrupt him or else he would talk all night long. Mom said it was OK to interrupt him if he had gone on for several minutes without stopping for a breath.)

"If that's really what you want to do, " said Mom. "It would certainly be nice to have all my questions answered."

"Mine too," said Becky, under her breath. But only Sam could hear her and only she could see him nod his head ever so slightly in agreement.

Chapter 11
LIGHTS OF THE NORTH

Later that night after everyone else was asleep, Becky was still tossing and turning in her bed. In the next room, Sam was snoring loudly. Becky was tired, but she just couldn't sleep. There were too many thoughts running around and around in her head. She snuggled deeper into the cozy comforter and tried to remember all the pieces to this puzzle of a day.

First there was Captain Pete's story about the ghost of Tom Adams and the shipwreck with the same name. Then there were the pleas for help and the note telling them to solve the riddle. Then there was the strange old woman telling them about the riddle on the outhouse door and Captain Pete losing his voice and not being able to tell anyone anything else about the ghost and…

Becky finally threw back the comforter and got out of bed. Even though it was the middle of summer, the air was cold, so she grabbed the quilt hanging over the rocking chair and felt around on the floor for her yellow, fuzzy slippers. Then she carefully made her way toward the lighter square of darkness that was the window.

AURORA BOREALIS
(ah-RoAR-ah bor-ee-AL-iss) The Northern Lights. Colorful bands of light sometimes seen in the night sky near the Arctic Circle.

It was after midnight in Michigan and everyone said this was the best time to see the **Aurora Borealis**—the Northern Lights. It was harder to see the lights during the summer, but sometimes you could.

Becky had never seen the Northern Lights—
even though she and her family had been in the
Upper Peninsula of Michigan for almost a week.
The first night they were here, she thought she saw
a faint glow low in the northern sky, but she didn't
think it was the mystical lights.

When she got to the window, Becky gasped.
There, right in front of her, green lights were
dancing in the sky. They made waves and wild
river-like swirls, bobbing up and down like yo-yos
on a string.

Becky rubbed her eyes, sure she was just imagining the dancing green lights. But they were still there—although never in the same place twice. They were teasing lights—gone one minute and then brighter than ever the next.

There was something totally fascinating about the Aurora Borealis. And even though these days everyone knew there was a scientific explanation for the lovely night lights, that didn't stop the show from being 100% magical.

Now, as much as Becky wanted to see the Northern Lights, she knew Sam wanted to see them even more. He had read eleven books about the Northern Lights (twelve if you counted the encyclopedia) and had seen two TV specials on public television that explained the mysterious show of lights.

Becky wanted to wake Sam, but she didn't want to leave the window and let the lights disappear. Finally it was too much, and she ran across the hall to get him. "Sam! Sam! Wake up! You've got to see this!"

"Go away Becky, I'm sleeping. Go 'way."

"Sam, it's the Northern Lights—they're out there and they're dancing. Come on!"

When he woke up enough to realize what Becky was saying, Sam practically fell out of his bed. He grabbed his fleece blanket and ran to the window. And then he just stared. "Wow! Look at them! I've never seen anything like this in my life! This is awesome!"

"Look Sam," said Becky softly, "they're just dancing. There's no music, no wind, no nothing, it's perfectly quiet, but they are dancing. You'd think that with all that movement there'd be music somewhere. But there's not. In fact, I'm even afraid to whisper because then that beautiful silence will be gone."

"Becky!" whispered Sam, "say that again. What you just said. Say it again!"

"I said I'm afraid to whisper because the beautiful silence would be gone. Why?"

Sam quoted, "'If you say my name I am gone.' If you say 'Silence' then the silence is gone. Becky, that's the answer to the riddle!"

Chapter 12
HE SPEAKS

Neither Sam nor Becky slept for the rest of that night. They watched the Northern Lights until almost dawn. By the time their parents got up, Sam and Becky were dressed and ready to go back to the lighthouse.

"Did you see them?" Sam could hardly wait to tell his parents about their nighttime adventures.

"Mom, Dad, did you see the Northern Lights last night? We did! We stayed up all night just watching them. They were beautiful and dancing and…"

"Whoa, boy!" said Dad. "Hang on a minute. So you saw the Northern Lights! That's great! Aunt Isabel said we might see them. I just never thought it would be this soon!"

"We'll tell you all about it on the trip over to the lighthouse," said Sam. "Let's go."

"Wait a minute, you guys. The first boat doesn't even start over until 9:30," said Mom. "Let's go have some breakfast. Ranger Leslie told us about a place that makes cinnamon rolls as big as plates!"

Sam smiled. Cinnamon rolls were his favorite. "Weeelll, as long as we can't go to the lighthouse any sooner, I guess a little breakfast would be good. *How* big are the cinnamon rolls?"

After breakfast (where Sam and Becky split a plate-sized cinnamon roll and told their parents all about the light show they had seen), they all boarded the *Virginia Gray* to return to the Copper Harbor Lighthouse. Captain Jack was at the helm again—Captain Pete still couldn't talk.

Last night, Becky and Sam discussed how they would reveal the answer to the riddle. "We *could* go to the outhouse," said Becky, "but somehow I don't think a ghost would be spending all eternity in an outhouse unless he had to."

"We could try the computer exhibit in the museum," offered Sam, "or the stairs to the tower in the lighthouse keeper's house."

"He does seem to hang out in a lot of different places," said Becky, "so maybe we should go back to the big rocks at the edge of the lake. That was the last place he tried to talk to us."

Sam had no better ideas, so he agreed.

Ranger Leslie met the *Virginia Gray* at the dock, and before they were even out of the boat, Mom and Dad started asking her questions. Sam and Becky walked as fast as they could out to the big rocks on the shore of the lake.

At the Copper Rocks (as Sam called them), Becky and Sam sat down on the biggest rock. "Should we just say the answer out loud or write it down on something?" asked Becky.

"Maybe we should do both—just to make sure."

"OK, you write it down and I'll say it out loud. Here—here's some paper and a pencil. Just write the word 'silence' on the paper and then fold it. Then, when I count to three, throw the paper in the water."

Sam quickly wrote the one-word answer to the riddle and looked up at Becky. "Ready," he said.

"Well, here goes."

In a loud voice Becky said, "Tom! Tom Adams! We know the answer to the riddle." She whispered to Sam, "One...two...three!" and then again loudly, "Tom, the answer is 'silence'."

Just as she said the word, Sam's paper—with the word "silence" written on it—hit the water beside the Copper Rocks.

Sam and Becky held their breath and looked around.

Nothing.

They strained their ears and listened.

The only thing they heard was the cry of the wild loons swimming in the lake, the lapping of the lake against the rocks, and the far-off sound of a passing ore boat. Then suddenly, *everything* was quiet. Even the loons and the lake and the boat were silent.

And then…softly, very softly, Becky thought she heard the tiny sound of somebody crying. The sound got a little louder and then there was a little sniffing sound.

"Are you crying?" Becky said out loud.

"No, I'm not. Boys don't cry."

"Sam, be quiet. I wasn't talking to you."

"And I wasn't talking to you, Becky. *I* didn't say that."

Becky and Sam looked at each other and their eyes got huge. Becky put her finger to her lips and then she said, "Tom? Tom Adams, is that you?"

"Well, who else would it be?" answered the voice. "I'm the only ghost around here—at least I think I am."

"Did you send us the notes?" asked Becky.

"Yes, I did," replied Tom. "Don't you think that was smart?"

"Did you get us wet in the boat with those big waves?" said Sam.

"Yes, I did. You two looked *so* funny. I thought I was going to die laughing…but, of course, I'm already dead…"

"Why didn't you just talk to us from the beginning? And where are you? Why can't we see you?"

"Well," said Tom, "that's kind of a long story. Are you sure you want to hear it?"

"Yes!" said Sam and Becky together.

So Tom began to tell his story.

Chapter 13
TOM'S STORY

"When I was 14," Tom began, "I wanted to be a sailor, but I was too young. I had a buddy who worked on a ship called the *Langham*, and he said he'd help me sneak aboard—I was a **stowaway**! "I decided to change my name so nobody would know who I was.

STOWAWAY
(STO-ah-way)
Someone who secretly gets on board a ship without the captain's permission.

"My buddy told me that when the *Langham* was first built, it was christened the *Tom Adams*, but it eventually got sold and the new owner changed its name to the *Langham*. So, when I sneaked aboard the ship, I decided to change my name to Tom Adams.

"My buddy tried to teach me some things about sailing, but it was tough to do without the crew seeing me. Mostly I did things at night when most of the sailors were asleep. It was hard, but I loved being on the water—I was finally a sailor!

"Pretty soon the sailors found me out, but they didn't seem to mind that I was a stowaway. I tried to help them whenever I could. Even the captain didn't mind my being on board.

"One day, we were on our way to Port Arthur up in Ontario with a load of coal when we ran into an awful storm. The wind was howling something fierce and I thought for sure the *Langham* was going to sink.

"But we didn't sink. We made it to Bete Grise Bay on the south side of the Keweenaw Peninsula, and all the crew and all the cargo were safe.

"Later that night, when everyone else had gone ashore to eat and celebrate, I was getting ready to go to sleep. I had made a little bed in a lifeboat that was actually pretty comfortable. All of a sudden, I saw this beautiful woman walking around on the deck. She had long, black hair and the most amazing green eyes.

"Well, I knew there was no woman with the crew, so I asked her what she wanted. I think I must have frightened her because she kind of jumped when I said something, and then she got angry. She mumbled something about looking for the captain, and the next thing I knew she was gone.

"I went back to the lifeboat, wrapped up in my blanket, and went to sleep. But I never woke up.

"Later I learned that the ship burned that night and I died in the fire. I don't remember anything about it except...I thought I saw that woman again.

"After I became a ghost, I decided that if I couldn't be a sailor, I'd try to help the sailors as much as I could. The sailors on the *Langham* had always been nice to me—even though I was a stowaway—and I wanted to do something nice for other sailors.

"The best thing about being a ghost was that I could help. I could move around and whisper in the captain's ear about a coming storm or put an "X" on a map to mark a dangerous area. I warned the navigators about rocks and other dangers, and—

just like a lighthouse—I helped guide ships into **port** when they couldn't see through the fog or a storm.

"It felt good to be doing something useful, but what I didn't know was that my helping the sailors was making someone else *very* angry.

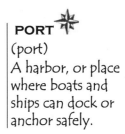

PORT
(port)
A harbor, or place where boats and ships can dock or anchor safely.

"One night there was a terrible storm. I used my powers and helped steer a ship back on course over near Bete Grise Bay. Later that same night, I appeared to the captain of a ship in Eagle Harbor to let him know that there was a bad leak in his engine room. After that, I saved a ship from crashing into the rocks right here off the lighthouse point. It was a really busy night!

"The strange thing was that every time I helped the sailors, there was this horrible noise. At first I just thought it was the storm getting worse, but after I saved the ship here in Copper Harbor, the noise got louder and louder until it turned into a screeching scream.

"Finally I realized that it was a *person* yelling and screaming. Then I saw a woman standing right here on top of the Copper Rocks—at least that's what I call them (Sam and Rebecca exchanged a smile). She was screaming at the top of her lungs…and she was yelling and screaming *at me!* That's when I realized this was the same woman I had seen on the *Langham* the night it caught fire.

"Boy, was she ever angry! She screamed that I better stop helping the sailors. She said she *wanted* the ships to hit the rocks and sink and that I was messing up all of her plans.

"Then her voice got really low and spooky. She told me her name was Malina and that she was a witch with great powers. She told me she was in love with the captain of the *Langham*, but he was not in love with her and would not marry her.

"Malina was furious! She vowed to get back at the captain by destroying his ship. So, she cast a spell and set fire to his ship as it sat in Bete Grise Bay. By morning, the *Langham* had burned and sunk to the bottom of the bay.

"I told her that I wasn't really a sailor, but had been a stowaway on the *Langham* and had died in that fire. She seemed pretty upset about that, and before I could say anything else, she closed her eyes, raised her arms up in the air, and chanted the same thing over and over. She said:

> *Hear my voice, oh magic tower,*
> *Take this boy's last drop of power,*
> *Voice and body from him take,*
> *Drown his magic in the lake,*
> *Entwine his gifts in riddles three,*
> *Another's aid the only key.*
> *From my curse now let him cower,*
> *Hear my voice, oh magic tower.*

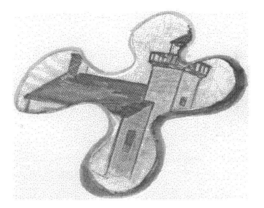

Chapter 14
A PIECE OF THE PUZZLE

"What the heck does that mean?" asked Sam breaking the silence.

"Well, I'm not sure," confessed Tom. "I didn't think about it much at the time because the storm was so bad and there was too much to do.

"I got away from the woman as fast as I could, and made my way over to Eagle Harbor where a ship was in trouble. But when I tried to warn the sailors, nobody could hear me—I had no voice! All I could do was let them see me and hope they could figure out that something was wrong.

⋇ AGROUND
(a-GROUND)
The bottom of a lake or other body of water. Ships usually "run aground" in the shallow waters near shore.

"Luckily the sailors were able to get their ship away from the shallow water before they ran **aground**.

"I still didn't really understand what was going on, but I didn't have time to figure it out because the storm was getting stronger. The rain was coming down hard and there was a ship about to wreck over near Bete Grise Bay.

"When I got there, I still had no voice and—to make matters worse—now I was invisible! They couldn't hear me and they couldn't see me. Then I realized that I didn't have any of my other powers either. I couldn't do *anything* to help!

"I had to watch that ship hit the rocks. Thank goodness, the sailors all made it to shore, but the ship sank in that storm.

"That's when I realized that Malina had put a curse on me. She had taken away my voice, made me invisible, and worst of all, she had taken away my special ability to know when a ship needed help!"

Tom was quiet for a minute and then in a low voice he said, "That witch was the cause of the wreck of the *Edmund Fitzgerald*. Twenty-nine sailors lost their lives when that ship went down. It was so awful...I should have been able to help them."

Sam and Becky could hear the sadness in his voice.

After a few minutes, Tom cleared his throat.

"Malina found me after the storm was over and she laughed at me. It was this really low laugh and it sounded really evil. She said, 'Since you can't talk, and nobody can see you, and you don't have any other powers, you won't be able to help

95

anyone— and no one will be able to help you.' Then she laughed again and just vanished. I never saw her again...until yesterday."

"You saw her yesterday?" Becky asked in surprise.

"Yes...at least I think I did, but it was a little strange. She was dressed up like an old woman, a nice grandmotherly type with a walking stick and white hair pinned up in a bun. But when I saw her eyes—those blazing green eyes—I knew it was that witch."

"She was carrying a walking stick carved like a cat wasn't she?" asked Becky excitedly. "Sam, that sounds like the woman who told us about the riddle in the outhouse! Do you think she was the witch?"

"But wait," said Sam, "if she put a curse on you, how can you be talking now?"

"Because you two solved the first riddle," said Tom, "so I got my voice back. By the way, did I ever say thanks? I'm not used to having a voice, so sometimes I forget to use it. Doesn't it sound wonderful? Thank you, thank you, thank you!"

"You're welcome, but we really didn't do that much," said Sam.

"I don't understand," Becky wrinkled her forehead as if she was trying to figure something out. "If it *was* Malina you saw yesterday, why would she help us find the answer to the first riddle? I mean, she's the one who put the spell on you in the first place, so why would she want us to solve the riddle?"

"That's true," said Sam. "It doesn't make sense that she would want to help you now. Maybe you were wrong—maybe it wasn't her."

"I don't know for sure that it was her," said Tom. But the woman I saw yesterday had the same green eyes as Malina. And if it *was* her, you two better watch out. She's not going to be very happy that you helped me get my voice back."

"So what *are* you going to do now that you have your voice back?" asked Sam.

"Well, right now I can only use my voice to help ships. When the rest of the spell is broken, I'll be able to let them see me and I'll have my other powers too. So, while I'm waiting for the next storm, I need to figure out how to break the rest of the spell."

"How much more is there?" asked Becky.

"Well," said Tom, if you listen to the curse, there are three parts. The first part took away my voice, the second part took away my body so no one could see me, and the third part took away all my other powers that I was using to help the ships and sailors. You helped me break the first spell and get my voice back. So now I need to figure out how to break the other two parts of the spell."

"But how do you know what to do to break the spell?" asked Sam.

"Well, I've spent a lot of time thinking about that," said Tom. "Copper Harbor was the place where I lost my voice and it's where you helped me find it. So, for the second part of the spell, I think I should go over to Eagle Harbor. That was the last place that anybody ever saw me. It's where I became invisible. Maybe I'll find something about a second riddle there. After that, I'll go back to Bete Grise Bay where I lost all my other powers.

"I have to say, though, it sure will be a lot easier to solve the other two riddles since I have my voice back. Thanks again for all your help. Being able to talk again is wonderful."

"You're welcome," said Sam and Becky together.

"It was really fun," Sam added with a grin.

"Sa-am! Be-cky! It's time to go."

"That's our mom," said Becky. She looked at Sam. "That must mean they've finished their research for the book. We should go."

"Well, don't forget to keep an eye out for Malina. I still think I saw her yesterday."

"Don't worry, Tom. If we see that old woman again we'll stay away from her."

"I know you will," said Tom, "but the problem is that she doesn't always look like that. When I first saw her, she was a beautiful young woman on the ship. And if the woman you talked to was really Malina, then she had changed to look like somebody's grandmother."

"So" said Sam, "we really don't know what— or rather who—to look out for when we're looking out for someone, right?"

"Confusing, but correct," said Tom. "She could be a beautiful young woman, a very old woman, a little girl, or anyone, anywhere in between."

"Rebecca! Samuel! Now!"

"We gotta' go, Tom! Good luck! Take care! Be careful!" Sam and Becky ran down the trail toward their mother's voice.

*****

The waves on Lake Superior lapped quietly at the Copper Rocks. In the distance, the sound of the *Virginia Gray* buzzing her passengers back across the harbor grew fainter and fainter. The loons were calling to each other from the edges of the lake, and in the midst of all the quiet noise, Sam and Becky thought they heard a very small voice say, "Thank you."

Chapter 15
WHAT'S NEXT?

"So, where are we going now?" asked Becky. She was still working on her ice cream cone (Yooper Delight this time—not Moose Tracks) as she got into the car.

"Yeah," said Sam, "which of the 116 lighthouses in Michigan are we going to visit next?" (He *was* eating Moose Tracks ice cream, but this time in a cup, not in a cone.)

"Well," said Dad, "we're actually just going up the peninsula a little way…up to the Eagle Harbor Lighthouse."

"That's right, said Mom. "Originally we had decided to skip that one and go a little farther west, but we bumped into a delightful elderly lady yesterday at the Copper Harbor Lighthouse who recommended that we not miss the lighthouse at Eagle Harbor. She practically insisted that we go there. How did she put it, Mike?"

"Wait, let me get it right. I remember because she said it in a very strange way. She said, 'There's a great deal to see there if you look at the right place.' It's almost like a riddle, isn't it?

"I tell you what, though," Dad continued, "she was in very good shape for a woman her age— very spry. She definitely did not need that walking stick she carried. And did you see her eyes? They were an amazing shade of green. Anyway, we thought we'd see what we could see at the Eagle Harbor Lighthouse. How does that sound to you guys?"

Becky looked at Sam and Sam looked at Becky. Their mouths were wide open, but they said absolutely nothing.

The End

Just So You Know

Remember I said there were lots of great books to read and websites to visit? Well, here are some of my favorites.

Books to Read

Berger, Todd R. and Daniel E. Dempster. *Lighthouses of the Great Lakes: Your Guide to the Region's Historic Lighthouses (Pictorial Discovery Guide),* Stillwater, MN: Voyageur Press, Inc., 2002.

O'Hara, Megan. *Lighthouse: Living in a Great Lakes Lighthouse,* 1910 to 1940, Mankato, MI:Capstone Press, 1998.

Penrose, Laurie et al. *A Traveler's Guide to 116 Michigan Lighthouses,* Davison, MI: Friede Publications, 1992.

Websites to Visit

"Copper Harbor, Michigan." <copperharbor.org>

"Exploring the North: The Upper Peninsula and Northern Wisconsin Traveler." <exploringthenorth.com/copper/copper.html>

"Seeing the Light: Lighthouses of the Western Great Lakes." <terrypepper.com/lights/superior/copper/copper.htm>

"LighthouseFriends.com." <lighthousefriends.com/light.asp?ID=226>

"Great Lakes Shipwreck Museum." <shipwreckmuseum.com> *(thanks, Andrew)*

Be sure to join
Becky and Sam in their
other
Michigan Lighthouse Adventures:

THE MYSTERY AT
EAGLE HARBOR

THE SECRET OF
BETE GRISE BAY